FOLK TALES RETOLD

SHANKAR

Children's Book Trust, New Delhi

Printed 1993
Reprinted 1995

Cover designed by Subir Roy

Revised combined edition

Text phototypeset in Times Roman

© by CBT 1993
ISBN 81-7011-697-X

Published by Children's Book Trust, Nehru House,
4 Bahadur Shah Zafar Marg, New Delhi, and printed
at its Indraprastha Press, New Delhi.

CONTENTS

A
MAN
OF
AN
ASS

Illustrated by P.S. Rau

ONCE there was a Maulvi in a village.
He had started a school in his own house.
Many children of the village came to the
school. There were several bright children
in it but there were some not so bright as
well. One day the Maulvi was very angry
with some of his students. He shouted at
them. "Do you know who I am? I have
made men out of asses and I know well
how to do that."

At that time a washerman was passing
by the Maulvi's house. He peeped into
the class just when the Maulvi was boast-
ing. The washerman heard what the
Maulvi said.

The washerman had no children but he had many asses. He ran home to his wife and asked her, "Did you know?"

His wife replied, "How could I know if you did not tell me."

"The Maulvi can make men out of asses," said the washerman. "I heard him say so with my own ears."

"How wonderful!" his wife said. "We have no children. Why not have one of our asses made into a man?"

"That is it," said the washerman. "that is why I ran home to tell you this. We will take our best ass, Moti, to the Maulvi and request him to change him into a man."

Next morning the washerman went to the Maulvi, saluted him and said, "Maulvi Saheb, I have no sons. But I have many asses. Will you change my best ass into a man? It will be of great help to me and to my wife."

The Maulvi was taken aback. "What are you saying?" he asked. "Can an ass ever be made into a man?"

"Don't say that, Maulvi Saheb," said the washerman. "I know you want to put me off. I know very well that you can do it. Please do help us."

The Maulvi tried to convince him that his request was an impossible one. But the washerman would not change his opinion. The Maulvi concluded that the washerman was a fool and he decided to treat him like one.

The Maulvi then said, "Listen, my friend. I don't do this kind of thing now, but your case is a special one. I shall take your Moti and change him into a man. But, changing an ass into a man takes time and money."

"How much will it cost, Maulvi Saheb?" the washerman asked eagerly.

"Oh, it will cost Rs.200 and take six months," said the Maulvi.

"Thank you, Maulvi Saheb," said the washerman. "I shall come with the money and the ass tomorrow."

The washerman hurried home to tell his wife about the clever bargain he had made. His wife was very happy that at

last they were going to have a son at home. They had saved enough and they could spare Rs. 200 for this. They did not want other people to know of the great miracle that was going to happen in their home.

The washerman took the ass and the money to the Maulvi next day and said, "Maulvi Saheb, here is your fees. Please make my Moti into a man."

The Maulvi took the money and asked the washerman to tie up the ass to a tree in his courtyard. "This is a beautiful ass," he said, "and I am sure the man made out of him will be a great man. Now you can go. Come after six months."

After the washerman left, the Maulvi asked one of his pupils to drive the ass far away into the jungle and leave it there.

Six months passed. The washerman went to the Maulvi with all hopes.

"My dear fellow, where have you been all this time?" the Maulvi enquired. "Your ass has become a learned man. He is now the Kazi of Varanasi. You better go there and see him."

"Will he recognise me when I meet him?" asked the washerman.

"Of course, he will," said the Maulvi. "But to make sure, you should take the gunny bag you used to feed him from. He will not forget the bag even if he has forgotten you."

The washerman went home and told his wife the whole story. They were happy that Moti was now a Government Officer. They wished to see him as soon as possible. The washerman decided to go to Varanasi immediately and bring Moti home.

Early next morning he set out on his journey.

In Varanasi, the Kazi was holding court when the washerman reached there. From a distance he saw the Kazi and was much impressed. 'What a clever man the Maulvi is!' He has changed Moti into such a great Kazi. So smart, learned and good-looking!' He waited for an opportunity to be seen by the Kazi. He moved to various positions and smiled and waved at the Kazi. But the Kazi was very busy and did not take any notice of him. Then he remembered what the Maulvi had said about the feeding bag.

The Kazi stopped writing and lifted his face from the desk. The washerman held up the feeding bag and smiled at him. He did this whenever the Kazi looked in his direction.

The Kazi saw what the washerman was doing. He became curious and sent for the man. The washerman was pleased and said to himself, 'At last the fool has recognised me.'

The Kazi asked him why he was there and what he wanted. The washerman felt hurt and shouted at the Kazi, "You don't know me, your own master? You ungrateful ass!" So saying he waved the feeding bag again and asked the Kazi, "Look at this. You don't recognise this bag from which you ate your corn everyday? Because the Maulvi has made you a man, you have forgotten your past! Come, Moti, let us go home. My wife is waiting for you."

The Kazi thought that all was not well
with the man and tried to talk to him with
sympathy. But this only made the washerman more impatient and angry.

So the Kazi ordered the courtiers to
drive him out. The washerman went away
shouting, "What an ungrateful ass he is!
I made a mistake in making him a man. He
was an ass and he should have remained
one. Is this justice of the land? I shall
show him what I am."

The washerman returned home and went straight to the Maulvi. He told the Maulvi the whole story. "Look what he has done to me after all that I have done for him. Please, Maulvi Saheb, please change him back into an ass. Take whatever fees you want. I must teach him a lesson."

The Maulvi laughed to himself. He demanded another Rs. 200 for changing the Kazi into an ass again. The washerman promised to come within a week with the money.

A week later the washerman went to the Maulvi's house with the money. In the meantime the Maulvi had brought Moti back from the jungle and tied it up in the courtyard of his house.

The washerman recognised him immediately.

"Do you now know who I am?" the washerman asked the ass. "You did not recognise me when I came to you. Now you will." So saying he rode home Moti, beating him all the way.

THE
KING'S
CHOICE

Illustrated by Reboti Bhusan

THERE was once a lion who was king of the forest. He was big and strong and very fierce.

All the other animals in the forest called him king. They brought him gifts from every corner of the forest.

But the more the lion had, the more he wanted.

'A king must have a court,' he said to himself one day.

He called a fox to his side.
"You are known to be a wise and
clever creature, fox," said the lion.
"I want you to be my adviser."
"Thank you, Your Majesty,"
said the fox, bowing low.

The lion next
called a leopard to
his side.

"You are known
to be watchful and
swift of foot,
leopard. I want
you to be my
bodyguard."

"Thank you,
Your Majesty,"
said the leopard,
bowing low.

The lion then called a vulture to his side.

"You are a bird, vulture, and can fly high. You are to be my messenger."

"Thank you, Your Majesty," said the vulture, bowing low.

The fox, the vulture and the leopard took an oath of loyalty to the king. The king promised to give them food and protection.

For some time all went well in the court of the lion king. The three courtiers never opposed the king. His wishes were law. Whenever he roared, they stood in awe. Whenever he took a walk, they followed him.

When the lion king went hunting, they found the animals for him to kill. And after he had had his meal, he left the remains for them. So they always had enough to eat.

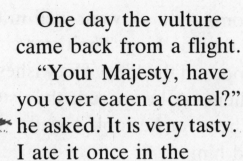

One day the vulture
came back from a flight.
"Your Majesty, have
you ever eaten a camel?"
he asked. It is very tasty.
I ate it once in the
desert."

The lion had never
seen a camel, but he liked the idea of
trying camel's meat.

"But where can we get a camel?" he
asked.

"There is a desert some miles away,"
said the vulture. "I was flying over it
when I saw a lone camel not far away. It
looked big and fat."

The lion looked at his other advisers. They were wise and experienced. He wanted their opinion. Now the fox and the leopard did not know the desert. But they did not want the vulture to seem wiser than them. So they said, since it was the vulture's idea, he should lead the way.

Early next morning the lion and his court started off on the camel hunt.

They reached the edge of the desert easily. But after they left the shelter of the forest, the day became very hot. The sun shone down with fire-hot rays.

High up in the cooler air the vulture flew.

"Hurry along," he called, "the camel is not far off."

But the lion could not hurry any more. The hot sand had burned his paws. He could go no farther.

"Stop!" he shouted to the others. "Let us go back to the forest. I do not care to try camel meat."

The lion king's advisers were frightened. The forest was far behind them and they did not know how to get the lion back home.

The leopard wanted to run away.

The vulture wanted to watch and wait and eat the lion later on.

But the clever fox thought of a plan. Off into the desert he ran saying, "I will bring some help."

After running for some time, the fox found the camel. The camel was indeed surprised to see him.

"Hurry up, friend camel," said the fox. "Our king wants you at once."

"Your king?" said the camel. "Who is
that? I do not know any king. I only
know my master, for whom I carry
goods across the desert."

"Our king, the lion, has killed your
master," said the fox. "Now you are
free, and the lion has invited you to live
at his court. Come along."

The camel followed the fox.

When the fox and the camel reached
the lion's camp, the vulture and the
leopard were surprised. Even the lion
looked pleased, in spite of his burned
paws.

The camel was presented to the king.
He agreed to serve the lion in return for
a home at his court.

"Get on the camel's back, Your Majesty," said the fox. "We will return home."

The lion at once jumped on to the camel's back. His courtiers, the fox and the leopard, jumped up behind him. And with the vulture flying ahead as a

guide, they set off on the long journey
back to the forest.

When the travellers reached the
forest, they were all tired and hungry.

The fox, the leopard and the vulture
looked at the camel. Then they looked
at each other and smiled hungry smiles.

They had brought the camel for the king's dinner. Now it was time for the feast.

The lion king knew what his courtiers were thinking. He called the camel to him.

"Friend camel," he said, "I have to thank you for saving my life. You are welcome to live at my court as long as you like. I promise you my protection."

The lion's courtiers were shocked. Had they not risked their lives so that he could try camel meat? And the king wanted to let the camel live!

The courtiers were not pleased with his decision. Yet they could do nothing.

Now the lion's paws were so badly burnt that he could not go hunting. But that did not keep him from growing very hungry indeed.

"Fox! Leopard! Vulture!" he shouted. "Don't you see that I am ill and hungry? Go and get me some food!"

The courtiers had to obey the king. So out they went. But they did not go far. They sat down in a safe place and discussed what they could do.

"I know," said the fox after a while, "we shall make the camel ask to be eaten."

He told the others of his plan.
They all agreed, so back they went
to the king.

First the vulture stepped forward.
"Your Majesty," he said, bowing
low, "we have found no food. But
we cannot let Your Majesty suffer.
I am a poor creature. Eat me."

The fox pushed the vulture aside, "I have more meat on me," he cried. "Eat me, Your Majesty."

Now the leopard rushed forward. "I am not much good," he cried. "But I could make a meal for the king."

The camel listened to all these offers. He must do as much, he thought.

"Your Majesty," he said. "I too am willing to give my life for you. Please eat me instead of these old friends of yours who will be more useful than I am."

This was what the fox, the leopard and the vulture were waiting for. They prepared to jump at the camel. But the lion stopped them.

"You are all good and loyal subjects," he said. "My heart is touched by your

offers. I accept them all. I shall eat you in the order in which you offered yourselves."

The vulture, the fox and the leopard were shocked.

Away flew the vulture. Away ran the fox and the leopard. They were never seen in the forest again.

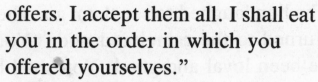

The lion laughed to see them go. Then he turned to the camel and said, "You have been loyal and good. You shall be my friend as long as we are alive."

The camel was happy and grateful. The lion thought to himself, 'To be king is good. But to be kind is better.'

THE
CLEVER
CALF

Illustrated by Reboti Bhusan

THIS is the story of a calf called Luthia. She was the prettiest little calf you could imagine, fawn-coloured, with great clear eyes. In fact, she had all the marks of a future Panchkalyani cow: she had rings of white above her hoofs; she had a white crescent mark on her forehead. Everybody liked her, and her master was proud of her.

The other farm animals loved Luthia, and were very kind to her. This was just as well for she had lost her mother when she was only twelve days old. Dhauli, the white cow, and Shyama, the black one, adopted her as their own, feeding her with their own milk, and licking her clean. The bullocks, Hira and Moti, and the big bull Parbat, were all very kind to her, taking great care of her, and guarding her with interest.

With everybody so fond of her, and no mother to correct her, Luthia became rather naughty. She was full of tricks. She bothered the bullocks when they were resting after a long day's work. She disturbed the cows in their sleep by licking their eyes or chewing their ears. Her favourite victim was the big bull, Parbat. She made faces at him, or pulled his tail, or jumped over him when he was asleep. Parbat was as strong as a giant, with a thick neck, and red eyes. He got very cross with Luthia. But he was tied strongly in his halter and was helpless against the teasing Luthia. He could only make angry noises and dig the ground with his hoofs while she stood a little way off and laughed at him. Still, Parbat really liked her, and sometimes joined in her frolics.

All the farm animals went out into the jungle every day to graze except Luthia who was left at home all alone. It seemed to her that the others were having great fun in the jungle, and she too

wanted to go and join in. She went to her master and asked him to let her go out with the others, and he agreed. So off she went into the jungle with them.

In this jungle there was a wily fox, who said he was the adviser and the best friend of the king of the forest, who is, as you all know, the lion. The fox pretended to represent the lion, and wanted all other animals to treat him as king. If anybody showed disrespect, the fox bullied him, and stopped him from grazing there. When any animal went to the forest for the first time, the fox expected the animal to go before him, bow down and pay homage.

Since Luthia was going to the jungle for the first time, the old cow Shyama warned her about the fox. Shyama told her that she should treat him like a real king, and be very, very respectful. "Is he really the king?" asked Luthia. "No," said Shyama, "he is only a fox, and he is a great nuisance and a trouble to us all. We have to pay homage to him to stop him bothering us." "Then I don't see why I should treat him like a king," said Luthia, "and I shall not."

When they went into the jungle, Luthia saw the fox sitting on a mound of clay, pretending it was a throne. Luthia thought this very funny, and couldn't help laughing. "Silence," shouted the fox. "Don't you realise, you silly little creature, that you are in the court of a ruler? Stop laughing this instant! Come and touch my feet and apologise."

Luthia pretended to be humble.

"I am sorry, my Lord, I didn't know you were so great; I thought you were an ordinary fox." "Will you or will you not come and pay homage to the representative of the great king, the lion?" asked the fox.

And do you know what Luthia said? She said. "I don't think you look anything like a king. You are just a silly fox, sitting on a mound of clay."

At this, all the other animals there started laughing and jeering at the fox. The fox was taken by surprise, and was quite at loss to know what to do. He would have liked to jump at Luthia and attack her, but as she was with all the other bulls and cows, the fox thought he had better not. He went angrily away, and swore to be revenged for his disgrace.

The fox decided to wait for an opportunity to kill Luthia, but there was no chance as she was always with the other stronger animals or in the farmyard. One night, he prowled around the farmyard, looking for a way to get in to kill Luthia. But as there was a strong fence all round, he could not get in. Luthia had seen him crouching outside, and she thought she would tease him.

"Who is there?" she asked. "Oh, I think it is an old cat. Perhaps waiting for a rat." The fox was very angry at this, but there was nothing he could do.

Having failed in his attempt to attack her, the fox decided to kill Luthia by cunning. He decided to make friends with her, and lure her out. He stood outside the farmyard one day, and called out, "Luthia, I admit you have won. We don't do any good by quarrelling. Let us make it up, and be friends. We could be good friends, you and I."

"How do I know I can trust you? asked Luthia. "How can anybody trust anybody else?" asked the fox. "We must show our love by trusting each other."

"Give me a little time to think it over," said Luthia. The fox said he would come back to know her decision and went away. But clever Luthia knew the fox was only trying to find another way to attack her. Going to Parbat, the strong bull, she said, "What a pity that such a strong friend as you can't help me against a little fox."

"What can I do?" asked Parbat. "The fox is light-footed and clever and would never come near me."

"I think you are afraid of the fox," said Luthia, trying to irritate him, "and I think the fox is more powerful than you!"

"No!" roared the bull. "No! I am not afraid. Just let him get near me, and I will show you what I will do to him!"

"All right," said Luthia, after thinking a minute, I will get the fox near you, but I hope you

will not be frightened and run away."

"No, I won't run away; I will tear him to pieces," he said. So when the fox came back the next night, Luthia said, "I think you really mean well, now, so let us be friends."

"That is a sweet little Luthia," said the fox, "come out and have a chat."

"Not so soon," she said. "Give me a little more time: come tomorrow night and wait outside for me. I will arrange for the gate to be kept open. You just sit under that tree with your back to me and keep your

eyes shut. Don't open them until I say 'Wake up, here comes your friend, Luthia.' If I see you peeping, I shall take it as cheating and go back."

The fox agreed to do as she wanted and promised to come back the next night.

Then Luthia told Parbat of her plan to get the fox wait for her with his eyes closed.

Next night the fox came and sat under the tree, waiting for Luthia to come. "Wake up, here comes your friend, Luthia," said Luthia, and the fox heard the sound of hoofs approaching. He thought he would soon have Luthia at his mercy and was delighted.

But it was Parbat who was coming up behind him. The fox heard heavy footsteps, and scenting danger, he looked round. But too late! Parbat rushed forward and charged, tossing the fox way, way up into the air. Then he came down plunk! He fell heavily and lay there a long time. Before daybreak he got up and limped away into the jungle. But after

some time he was ashamed even to stay in that jungle and left for a place, far, far away.

And all the animals rejoiced that the wily fox had been driven away from the jungle by the clever Luthia.

A
WOMAN'S
WIT

Illustrated by Shankar

VISHNU Potti was the pujari of a temple in Kerala. He lived with his wife in a small house. He was poor. But he wanted to be charitable. Therefore, everyday he took home some stranger with him to share his food though he could not afford to do so. He thought it was his duty to share with others what he ate.

His wife, Laxmi, did not like this. But she was a loving wife and did not want to do anything against her husband's wishes. Many a time she had to give her share of the food to the guests. At such times, Laxmi had to go hungry.

Laxmi tried to manage the house as well as she could. Often she had to borrow rice or vegetables from the neighbours. At times, she had even to beg. This cannot go on, she thought. The neighbours were getting angry with her. They did not believe she was poor, for they saw her feeding guests every-day. Laxmi had nobody to help her. She went hungry for days. Life became a burden to her.

At last, Laxmi felt that she could not bear it any longer. She decided to talk things over with her husband.

One night, after dinner, Vishnu Potti was about to go to bed. Laxmi went up to him and said she had something to tell him. He was taken aback. Never before had she talked to him thus. He sat down on the bed.

Laxmi started crying. She could not speak for some time. Her husband became impatient. At last, wiping her eyes with the end of her sari, she said, "We have guests everyday. It is good that we share our food with others. But have you ever cared to find out if we have enough to feed them? We are poor and the food we have is hardly enough for us. Where shall I find food for the guests? They always get my share of the food and I am left to starve. I cannot put up with this any more. Have pity on me, my lord, and help me. Don't invite any more guests to our home."

Vishnu Potti was shocked. How dare his wife tell him not to bring guests home! Did she not love him any longer? Perhaps, he thought, she did not know what she was saying. She had said something foolish, and maybe, she would feel sorry for it.

He called her to his side, patted her on the back and said, "Don't cry. I forgive you your foolishness. We are doing good when we share our food with others. Any sacrifice you make will be for my good. If you die because you gave your food to others, you are sure to reach Heaven before I do. Have faith in God and do your duty to your husband."

So saying, he lay down on his bed and was soon fast asleep.

Laxmi could not sleep a wink. She wept quietly to herself, wondering what to do. She could see no way out of her misery.

The pujari rose the next morning and went to the temple. He came home for lunch as usual with a couple of strangers. Laxmi saw them from afar, coming down the pathway. She felt miserable. Suddenly she had an idea.

Vishnu Potti and his guests reached home. He asked them to sit down while he went to have a wash. When he was gone, Laxmi took the large wooden pestle which she used to husk paddy and leaned it against the wall. After that, she lit a brass lamp and put flowers on the pestle. Then she sat before it as if in prayer, where the guests could see her. They saw her and were puzzled. It was odd to see a woman worshipping a pestle. They wanted to know why she was doing so.

They came closer to her, and stood watching her for some time. She appeared lost in prayer. Then slowly, she lifted her head and turned to them. She looked frightened.

"Please tell us," they asked, "why do you worship this pestle?"

Tears came to Laxmi's eyes. She told them that she was not free to say anything against her husband. "It concerns you, but you must not know it," she said.

This made the guests all the more anxious to know what it was all about. "We must know if it concerns us," they said.

"Promise me that you will not tell my husband."

"We promise," said the guests.

Laxmi said, "My husband is a kind man. He brings guests home for a meal, but beats them with this pestle after he has fed them. He thinks it is his sacred duty to do so. I serve them food but I don't want anything to do with the beating. I am doing puja before the pestle so that I may be free from the sin."

The guests looked at each other and thought it

wise to leave before their host returned. When Vishnu Potti came back, he asked his wife where his guests were.

She answered sadly, "Forgive me my foolishness. They wanted me to give them this pestle as a gift. You know we have only one in the house, and I told them I could not. They got annoyed and left."

Vishnu Potti was angry and shouted at his wife, "How dare you insult my guests? Give me the pestle."

He snatched the pestle from her hand, and ran after the guests, who were by now far down the path. The guests saw the angry pujari coming after them with the pestle.

"He is coming to beat us!" they screamed and broke into a run. They ran faster and faster. Vishnu Potti could not overtake them and he had to turn back.

The villagers saw Vishnu Potti running after his guests. They thought he was chasing them away. The guests told everybody that the pujari took guests home only to beat them up with the pestle. Soon the story spread far and wide. No one came to eat with Vishnu Potti anymore.

And Laxmi no longer went without food.

THE
BEGGAR
KING

LONG ago there was a king named Anup Singh. His kingdom was called Anupnagar.

King Anup Singh was very rich. He had many palaces and many servants. He was very ambitious. He kept a large army. He often fought with his neighbours and expanded his kingdom.

The king was fond of hunting. It was his favourite sport. One day he decided to go on a hunt. He started with a large party of attendants for the jungle where they expected good game. The jungle was far away. They were riding on fine, mettlesome horses.

When they reached the jungle the day was well advanced. For hours they rode through the jungle without coming across any game. Then, at last, they sighted a deer. The king set his horse at it. The deer ran at great speed and the king followed. It was a long chase. In the end the deer escaped.

King Anup Singh was disappointed. He was tired and wanted to get back to his companions. But they had been left far behind. The king had lost his way. He shouted for his attendants at the top of his voice, but there was no reply. The king wandered in the jungle for a long time hoping to find a way out. The day was almost over and darkness was setting in. The king was worried.

He wanted to get out of the jungle before it was night. He directed his horse on a straight course and rode on.

Soon it was night and there was no moon. The king could not see anything. He hoped his horse would carry him out of the jungle. The horse went on and on, and finally the king came out of the jungle.

He looked around. There was no village to be seen anywhere. The sky was covered with dark clouds and it started raining. It would be difficult to return to the palace that night, thought the king. He decided to take shelter in some village.

He did not know where he was. His horse, however, continued to go forward.

At last the king saw a light. He was happy and moved in the direction of the light. It was a village. The king stopped at the first house and knocked at the door. It was a farmer's house.

"Who is it?" asked a voice from inside.

"A traveller seeking shelter for the night," said the king.

The farmer's wife opened the door and asked the king to enter. The farmer welcomed the visitor respectfully and said, "Please consider this as your house. Make yourself comfortable. It is our good fortune that we have a guest at times."

The king did not tell them who he was. He said he was a royal messenger returning to the city after a long journey, that he could not proceed further because of the rain and darkness.

The farmer said, "A guest is a guest, whether he is a messenger or a king. We shall do our best to be of service to our guest."

The farmer took out some clothes and gave them to the visitor to change, and said, "Remove your wet clothes and take some rest. My wife will give you food while I go and look after your horse."

The farmer's wife prepared the meal. It was simple, but the king was very hungry and he ate it with relish. The farmer made a bed for the guest. The king lay down and soon fell asleep.

The king got up early next morning. But the farmer and his wife were up even earlier and had milk and fruit ready for him.

The king was very pleased with the welcome he had at the farmer's house. He thanked the farmer and his wife for what they had done. He took out a piece of paper from his pocket, wrote something on it and handed it over to the farmer and said, "If ever you are in difficulty or in need, come to the city and show this chit to anyone there. You will get whatever help you want."

Then the king took leave of them, mounted his horse and rode away. The farmer stood staring after the king in astonishment and dropped the little piece of paper. But his wife picked it up and put it safely in a box.

Years passed. The farmer and his wife continued to live happily. There was enough rainfall every year, the crops were always good, and they grew more and more prosperous.

Then came drought, parching the brown land.
Famine followed. People starved, cattle died, and
the whole village was on the verge of ruin.

The farmer's wife remembered then the little piece
of paper that she had kept in the box. She reminded
her husband of it. The farmer was not happy about
going out and seeking help; but the whole village
was hungry, and so he decided to go to the city and
try his luck.

Early next morning the farmer took the chit and started for the city. He had to walk a long distance to reach it. He grew very tired. He sat down under a tree to rest and soon fell asleep.

He was roused from sleep by someone shouting. He looked up and saw a policeman in front of him. The policeman ordered him to go away.

The farmer then took out the piece of paper and showed it to him.

The policeman looked at the chit, immediately bowed, and requested the farmer to follow him. He took the farmer to the gate of the royal palace and whispered something to the guard. The guard then took the farmer into a splendid courtyard and entrusted him to an officer. The officer took him to a beautiful marble temple. At the door of the temple the officer asked the farmer to go straight in; inside was the king whose chit he had in his hand.

The farmer was astonished to see that it was the king who had stayed with him as a guest. The king was inside the temple, praying.

"O, Almighty," the king said, "I am grateful to you for all that you have given me. I want more. Give me more and more—give me all things—and bless me."

The farmer heard the king pleading and begging. He turned back and quickly walked out of the temple and out of the splendid palace courtyard. At the gate he threw away the piece of paper and walked back the long way home.

The guard saw the paper lying near the gate. He took it to the king.

"Where is he?" the king demanded. "Bring him in immediately."

But the farmer had gone, and was not to be found anywhere. The king was furious. He blamed his servants in the palace for sending the farmer away. He decided to go to the farmer himself and find out what he wanted.

The king started with a large party for the farmer's village. It was midnight when they reached there. There were no lights in the village and it took some time for the king's party to find the farmer's house.

At last the king found the farmer and his wife. He asked the farmer why he had returned without seeing him.

The farmer said, "I came to beg for your help. I saw you praying in the temple. There you were on your knees, begging God to give you more. I then thought you were a bigger beggar than I. Therefore I could not expect anything from you—and so I came away."

The king stood still for a while, thinking. Suddenly, he touched the farmer's feet and asked for his forgiveness. He then turned to his companions and ordered immediate help not only to the farmer and his family, but to all the other people who suffered because of the famine.

Other CBT Titles By The Author

MAHAGIRI

LIFE WITH GRANDFATHER

THE WOMAN AND THE CROW

FOUR DEAF MEN

FOOL'S PARADISE

THE LION AND THE RABBIT

THE TORTOISE AND THE SWANS

THE LOYAL MONGOOSE

SUJATA AND THE WILD ELEPHANT

THE MONKEY AND THE WEDGE
AND ANOTHER STORY